Under the Dancing Tree

Endorsements

Under the Dancing Tree is a beautiful depiction of a daddy's love for his little girl. I teared up just thinking of my girls with their daddy. I love to see Chip's love for his daughters through his words. Chip perfectly portrays what a daddy's love looks like as his little girl grows. This book is a must-have for anyone with daughters!
　　—Tiffany Nardoni, author of *Still* (when all else fades away)

Under the Dancing Tree takes readers on the playful journey of childhood. Parents will finish this book with a deeper appreciation for the moments that create the memories—a powerful reminder to enjoy the details along the way. Sure to be a favorite among fathers and daughters of all ages.
　　—Seth Miller, PhD, superintendent of Westville School District #2

Every parent knows we raise our children to grow up and leave the 'nest.' Few of us look forward to that day. The story of the magical, memory-making Dancing Tree shows a dad's enduring love for his daughter from newborn to childhood and toward a hope-filled future once she's grown. Thanks, Chip, for encouraging us to celebrate the small ordinary moments—and to joyfully anticipate every moment that comes next with our own children.
　　—Lori Hensold, B.S., M.Ed., empty-nest mom to six grown children, five grandchildren

I have known Chip Mattis for many years, and I have had the privilege of watching him raise his children. Chip cares deeply for his kids, and a book like this touches on the deep relationship between a father and his daughter. As a pastor and father of five girls, I think *Under the Dancing Tree* would be an excellent keepsake to buy for a child or even later in life to give as a wedding gift.
　　--Mac McElhaney, Lead Pastor, Rolling Hills Vineyard Church

Under the Dancing Tree

Chip Mattis

PUBLISHING THE POSITIVE

ELK LAKE PUBLISHING INC
Plymouth, Massachusetts

Copyright Notice

Under the Dancing Tree

Cover and Interior Design: Derinda Babcock

Illustrator: Doan Trang

Editor: Deb Haggerty

Author Represented by Golden Wheat Literary

PUBLISHED BY: Elk Lake Publishing, Inc., 35 Dogwood Dr., Plymouth, MA 02360, 2019

Library Cataloging Data

Names: Mattis, Charles "Chip" (Charles "Chip" Mattis)

Under the Dancing Tree / Charles "Chip" Mattis

32 p. 216 mm × 216 mm (8.5 in × 8.5 in.)

Description: A father remembers the special times with his daughter "under the dancing tree."

Identifiers: ISBN-13: 978-1-950051-03-8 (Trade Hardback) | 978-1-950051-16-8 (Trade Paperback) 978-1-950051-04-5 (POD) | 978-1-950051-05-2 (e-book)

Key Words: Fathers, Daughters, Growing Up, Memories, Family, Relationships, Inspirational

LCCN: 2019932680 Fiction

Dedication

To Jessie who is my biggest supporter.

To Brian and Sandy who love this orphan boy.

To Olen who is an honoring and caring young man.

And most of all to Sophie and Charlotte who are growing entirely too fast.

Back before I met you,

There was just one girl for me—

Resting our heads in the front yard grass

Under the shady tree.

Then a few years later,

You came and made us three—

Rocking you in our arms to sleep

Under the breezy tree.

Now you like to run around

And jump and spin with glee.

You grab a hanging branch and twirl

Under the dancing tree.

I hang a seat from an upper limb

For a swing, and you say, "Whee!

Daddy, I can touch the sky!"

You can from the swinging tree.

Someday, you'll begin to reach

And call for me to see

You're strong enough to scramble up

Into the climbing tree.

Spring will come with flowers.

You'll wear one just for me.

We'll watch as petals drop around us

Under the blossom tree.

I'll spend hours every autumn

Raking leaves into a pile.

So, you can jump and scatter them,

Which I intended all the while.

And one day you will grow up big

And find your husband-to-be.

Tears will surely fill my eyes,

But a smile is all you'll see.

I'll think of all the times before ...

And all the times to be ...

Always ready to see you here

Under our dancing tree.

Chip Mattis

FROM THE TIME HE WAS SMALL, CHIP LOVED TO READ AND WRITE. He wrote poems for his grandmother and songs for himself. As a sophomore in high school, Chip won a contest to have a poem published in an anthology of U.S. high school poets. It was a seminal moment.

A few years later, Chip was admitted to the collegiate poetry and short story club, Scribblerus. He was dedicated to the purpose of the club: to read and critique others' work in the club and submit works for critique by others. They met every week, and the honing of his craft began in earnest. He graduated magna cum laude from Greenville University with a BA in Philosophy and Religion.

Chip attended the Blue Ridge Mountain Christian Writers Conference in 2018 where he was awarded the Foundations First Runner-Up for Best Children's Picture Book. His debut book, *Under the Dancing Tree*, from Elk Lake Publishing will be in stores in 2019.

CPSIA information can be obtained
at www.ICGtesting.com
Printed in the USA
LVHW070445110620
657820LV00002B/10